TRANSFORMERS: ALLIANCE
ISSUE NUMBER THREE (OF FOUR)

WRITTEN BY: **CHRIS MOWRY**
ART BY: **ALEX MILNE**
COLORS BY: **JOSH PEREZ**
LETTERS BY: **CHRIS MOWRY**
EDITS BY: **DENTON J. TIPTON**

When the DECEPTICON known as WRECKAGE is revived from a fragment from the ALLSPARK, he destroys the SECTOR SEVEN base in the Nevada desert only to be killed by the vengeful warrior STARSCREAM. Though many human lives are lost, many more are saved thanks to the heroic efforts of BUMBLEBEE. With SECTOR SEVEN gone, there has come a time for unity between the humans and AUTOBOTS. Their alliance could not have come sooner. For out in space, the mysterious SOUNDWAVE has summoned the DECEPTICON forces.

Special thanks to Hasbro's Aaron Archer, Michael Kelly, Amie Lozanski, Val Roca, Ed Lane, Michael Provost, Erin Hillman, Samantha Lomow, and Michael Verrecchia for their invaluable assistance.

To discuss this issue of *Transformers*, join the IDW Insiders, or to check out exclusive Web offers, check out our site:

 Licensed by:

VISIT US AT
www.abdopublishing.com

Reinforced library bound edition published in 2010 by Spotlight, a division of the ABDO Group, 8000 West 78th Street, Edina, Minnesota 55439. Published by agreement with IDW Publishing. www.idwpublishing.com

Printed in the United States of America, Melrose Park, Illinois.
102009
012010

 PRINTED ON RECYCLED PAPER

Library of Congress Cataloging-in-Publication Data

Mowry, Chris.
  Alliance / written by Chris Mowry ; art by Alex Milne ; colors by Josh Perez & Kris Carter ; letters by Chris Mowry & Neil Uyetake.
     v. cm.
  "Transformers, revenge of the fallen, official movie prequel."
  ISBN 978-1-59961-717-6 (vol. 1) -- ISBN 978-1-59961-718-3 (vol. 2)
  ISBN 978-1-59961-719-0 (vol. 3) -- ISBN 978-1-59961-720-6 (vol. 4)
  1. Graphic novels. I. Milne, Alex. II. Transformers, revenge of the fallen (Motion picture) III. Title.
  PZ7.7.M69Al 2010
  741.5'973--dc22

                              2009036393

All Spotlight books have reinforced library bindings and are manufactured in the United States of America.

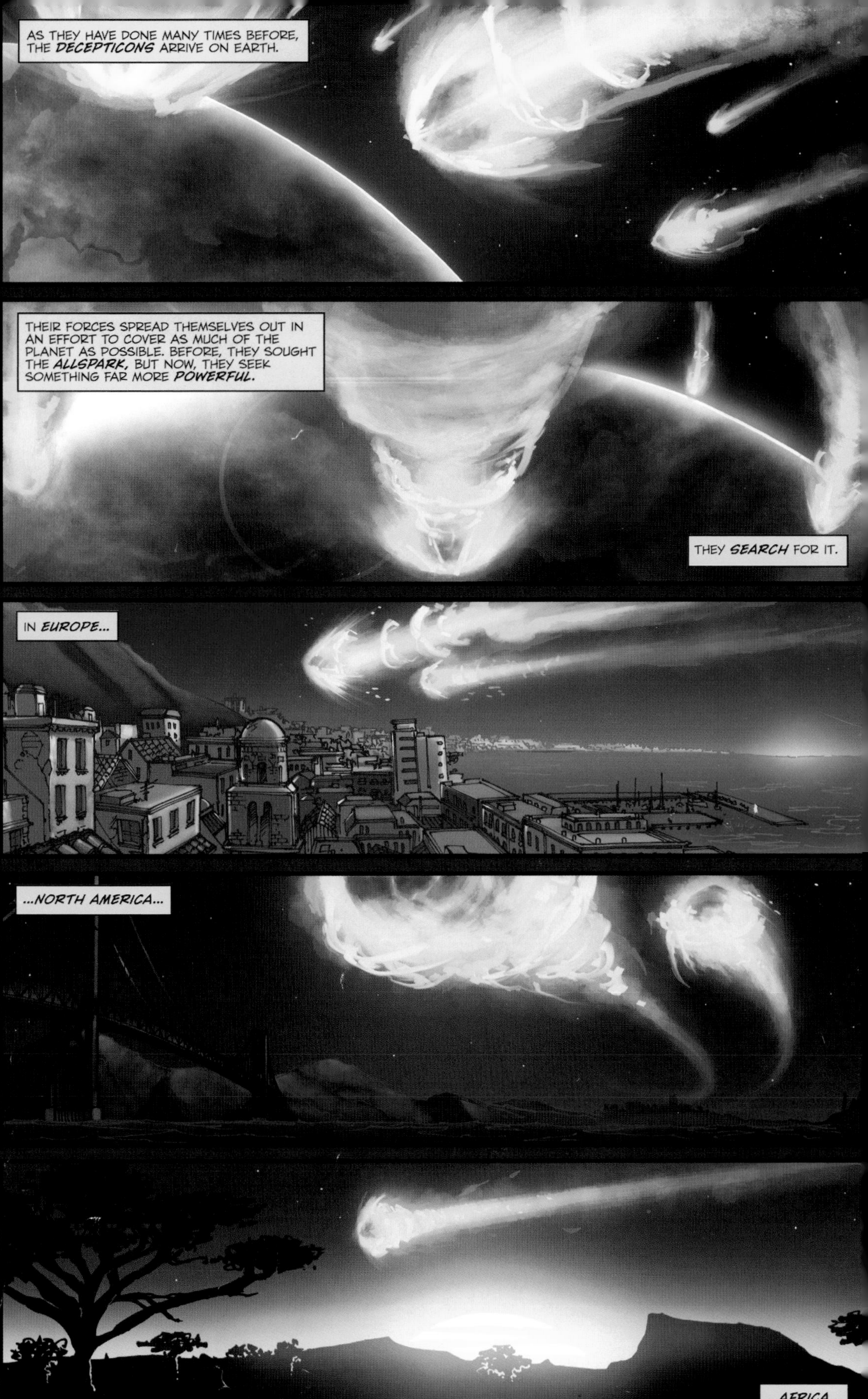
AS THEY HAVE DONE MANY TIMES BEFORE, THE DECEPTICONS ARRIVE ON EARTH.
THEIR FORCES SPREAD THEMSELVES OUT IN AN EFFORT TO COVER AS MUCH OF THE PLANET AS POSSIBLE. BEFORE, THEY SOUGHT THE ALLSPARK, BUT NOW, THEY SEEK SOMETHING FAR MORE POWERFUL.
THEY SEARCH FOR IT.
IN EUROPE...
...NORTH AMERICA...
...AFRICA...

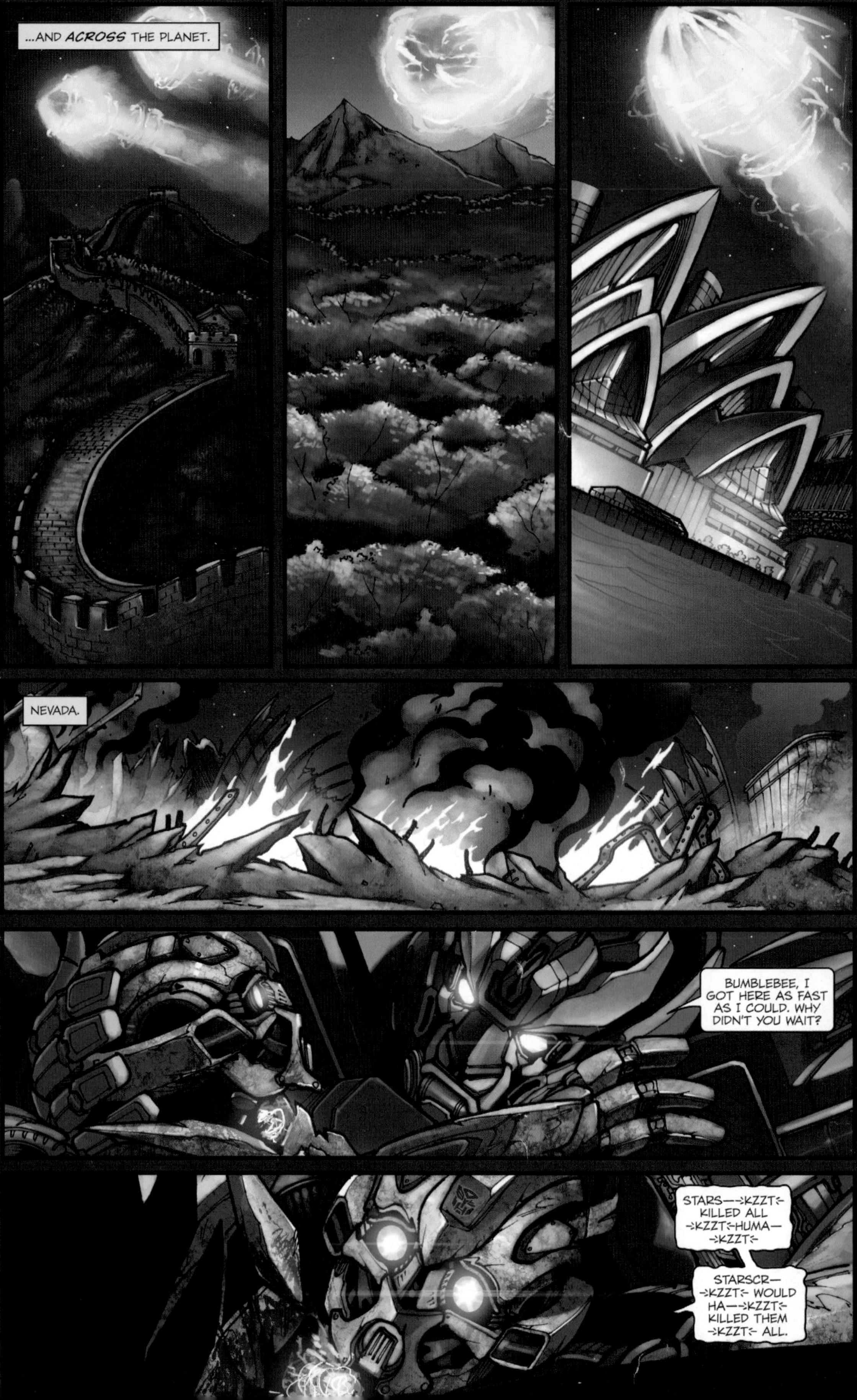
...AND ACROSS THE PLANET.
NEVADA.
BUMBLEBEE, I GOT HERE AS FAST AS I COULD. WHY DIDN'T YOU WAIT?
STARS— -KZZT- KILLED ALL -KZZT- HUMA— -KZZT-
STARSCR— -KZZT- WOULD HA— -KZZT- KILLED THEM -KZZT- ALL.

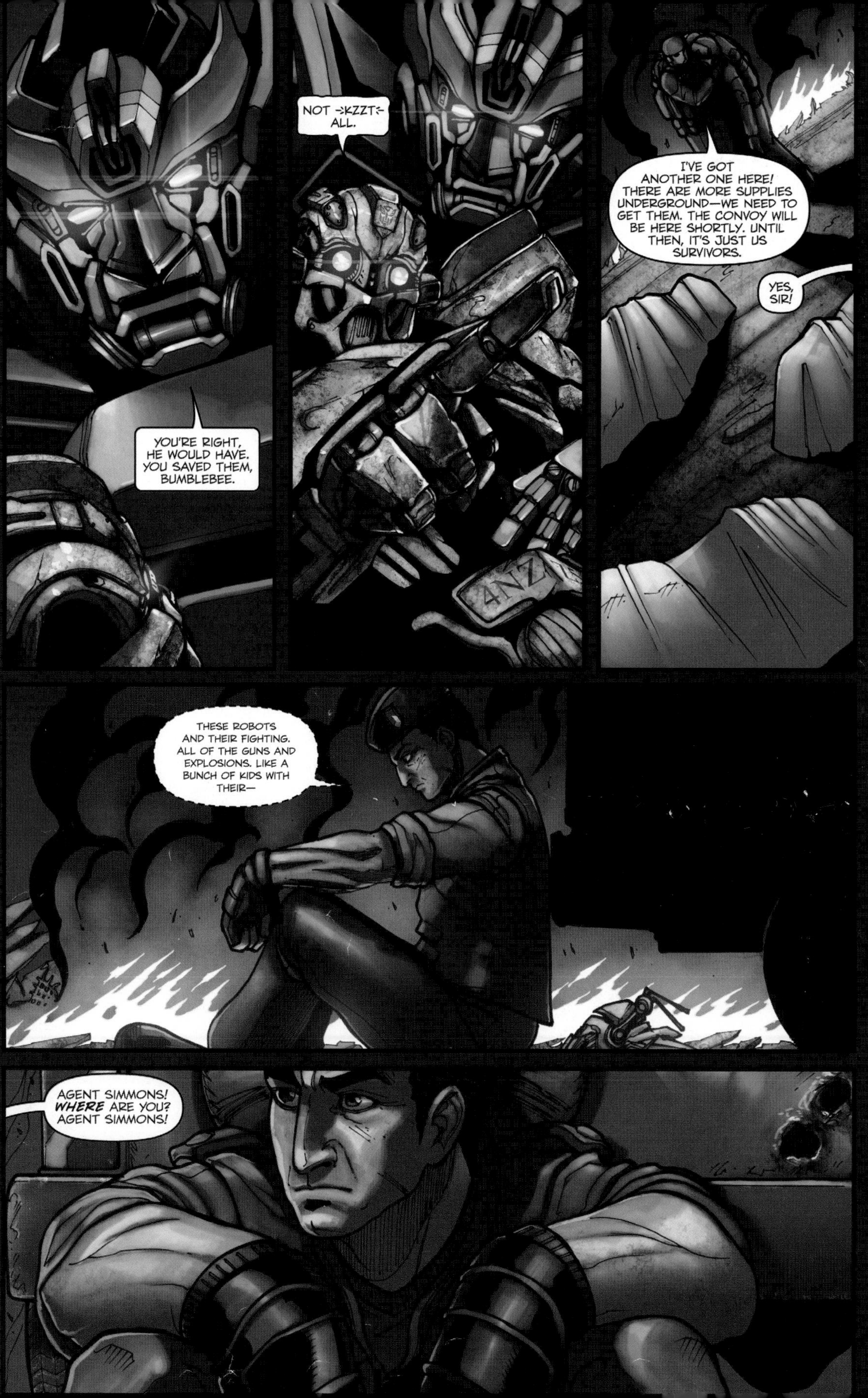
YOU'RE RIGHT, HE WOULD HAVE. YOU SAVED THEM, BUMBLEBEE.
NOT -KZZT- ALL.
I'VE GOT ANOTHER ONE HERE! THERE ARE MORE SUPPLIES UNDERGROUND—WE NEED TO GET THEM. THE CONVOY WILL BE HERE SHORTLY. UNTIL THEN, IT'S JUST US SURVIVORS.
YES, SIR!
THESE ROBOTS AND THEIR FIGHTING. ALL OF THE GUNS AND EXPLOSIONS. LIKE A BUNCH OF KIDS WITH THEIR—
AGENT SIMMONS! WHERE ARE YOU? AGENT SIMMONS!

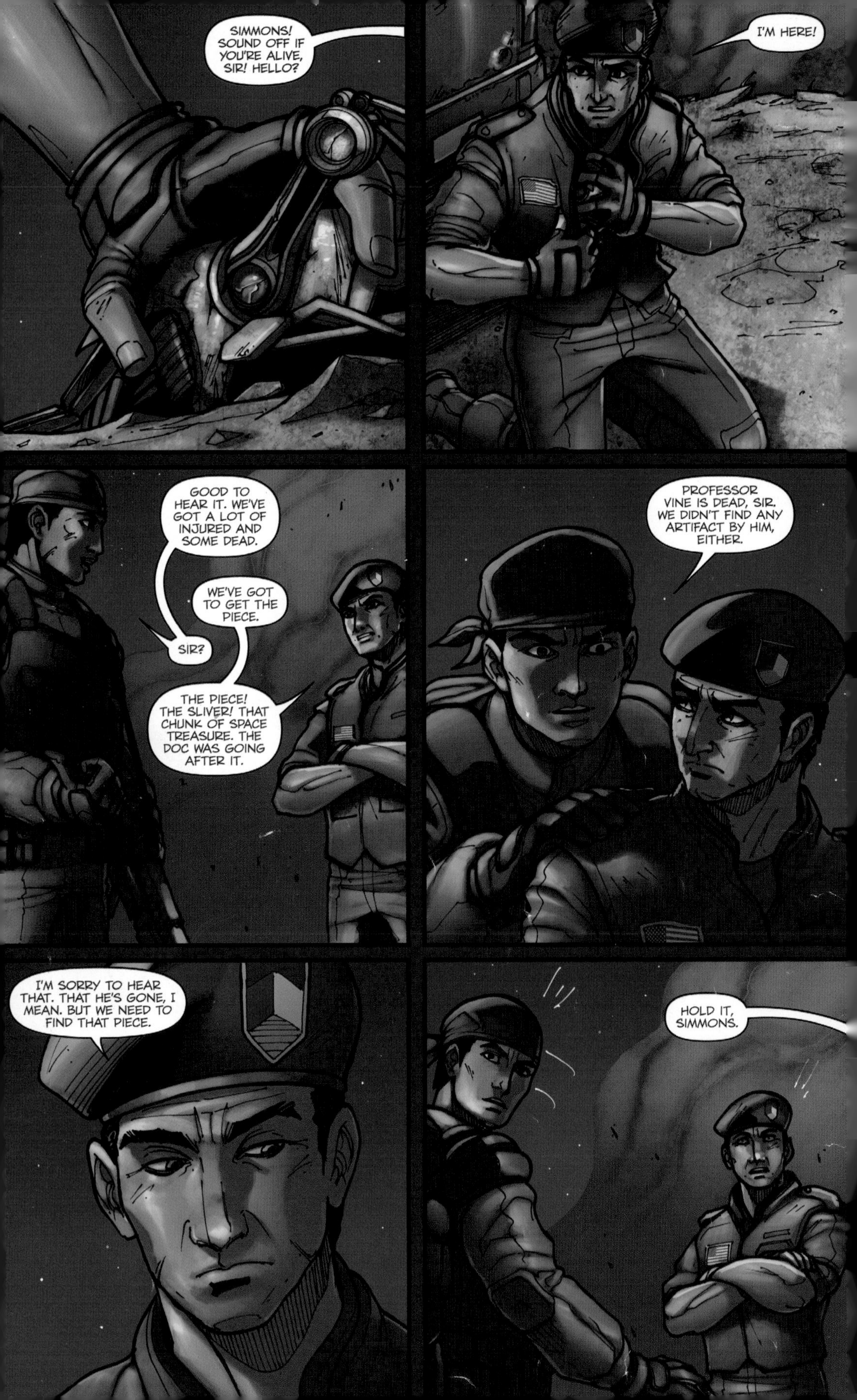
SIMMONS! SOUND OFF IF YOU'RE ALIVE, SIR! HELLO?
I'M HERE!
GOOD TO HEAR IT. WE'VE GOT A LOT OF INJURED AND SOME DEAD.
SIR?
WE'VE GOT TO GET THE PIECE.
THE PIECE! THE SLIVER! THAT CHUNK OF SPACE TREASURE. THE DOC WAS GOING AFTER IT.
PROFESSOR VINE IS DEAD, SIR. WE DIDN'T FIND ANY ARTIFACT BY HIM, EITHER.
I'M SORRY TO HEAR THAT. THAT HE'S GONE, I MEAN. BUT WE NEED TO FIND THAT PIECE.
HOLD IT, SIMMONS.

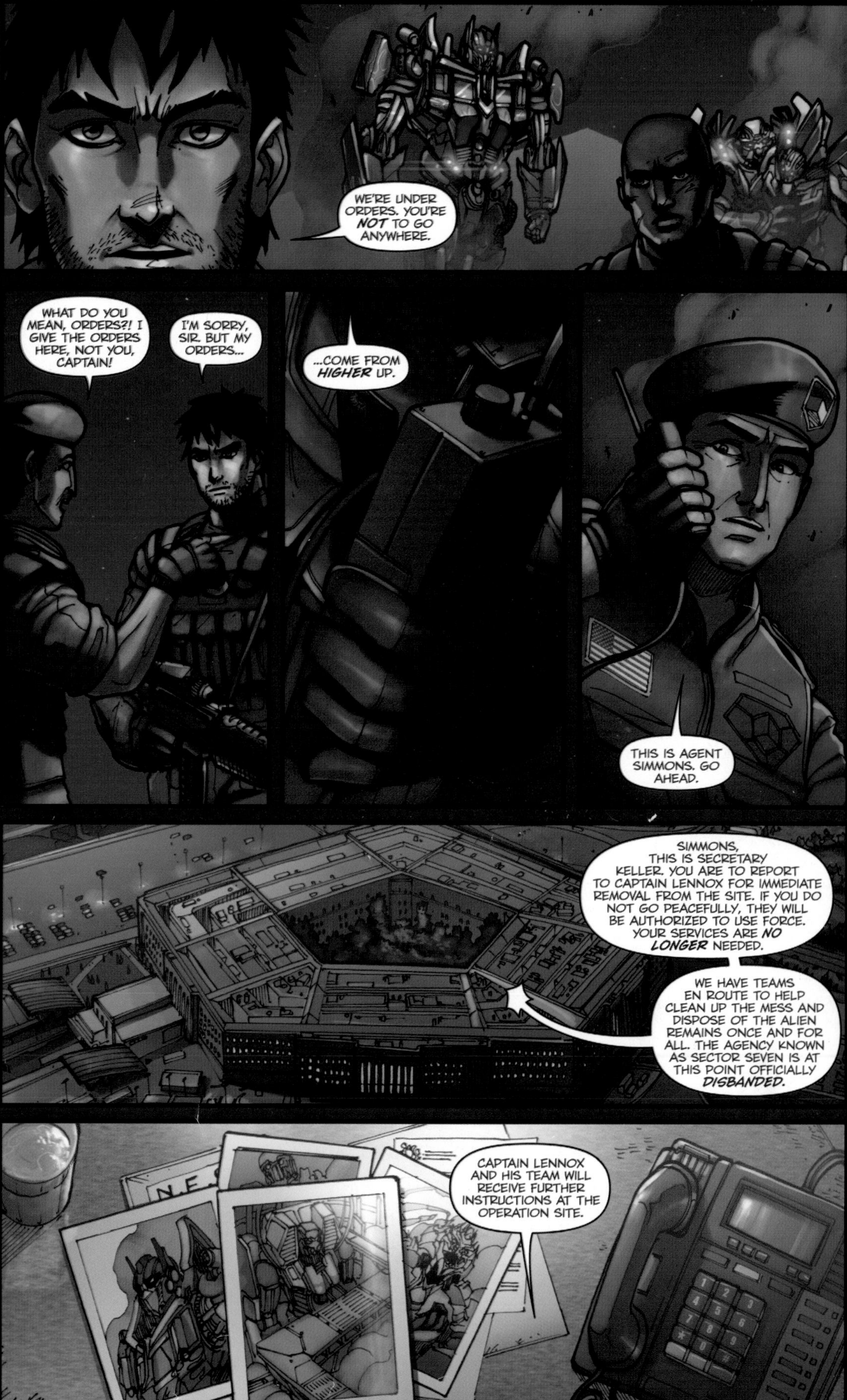
WE'RE UNDER ORDERS. YOU'RE NOT TO GO ANYWHERE.
WHAT DO YOU MEAN, ORDERS?! I GIVE THE ORDERS HERE, NOT YOU, CAPTAIN!
I'M SORRY, SIR. BUT MY ORDERS...
...COME FROM HIGHER UP.
THIS IS AGENT SIMMONS. GO AHEAD.
SIMMONS, THIS IS SECRETARY KELLER. YOU ARE TO REPORT TO CAPTAIN LENNOX FOR IMMEDIATE REMOVAL FROM THE SITE. IF YOU DO NOT GO PEACEFULLY, THEY WILL BE AUTHORIZED TO USE FORCE. YOUR SERVICES ARE NO LONGER NEEDED.
WE HAVE TEAMS EN ROUTE TO HELP CLEAN UP THE MESS AND DISPOSE OF THE ALIEN REMAINS ONCE AND FOR ALL. THE AGENCY KNOWN AS SECTOR SEVEN IS AT THIS POINT OFFICIALLY DISBANDED.
CAPTAIN LENNOX AND HIS TEAM WILL RECEIVE FURTHER INSTRUCTIONS AT THE OPERATION SITE.

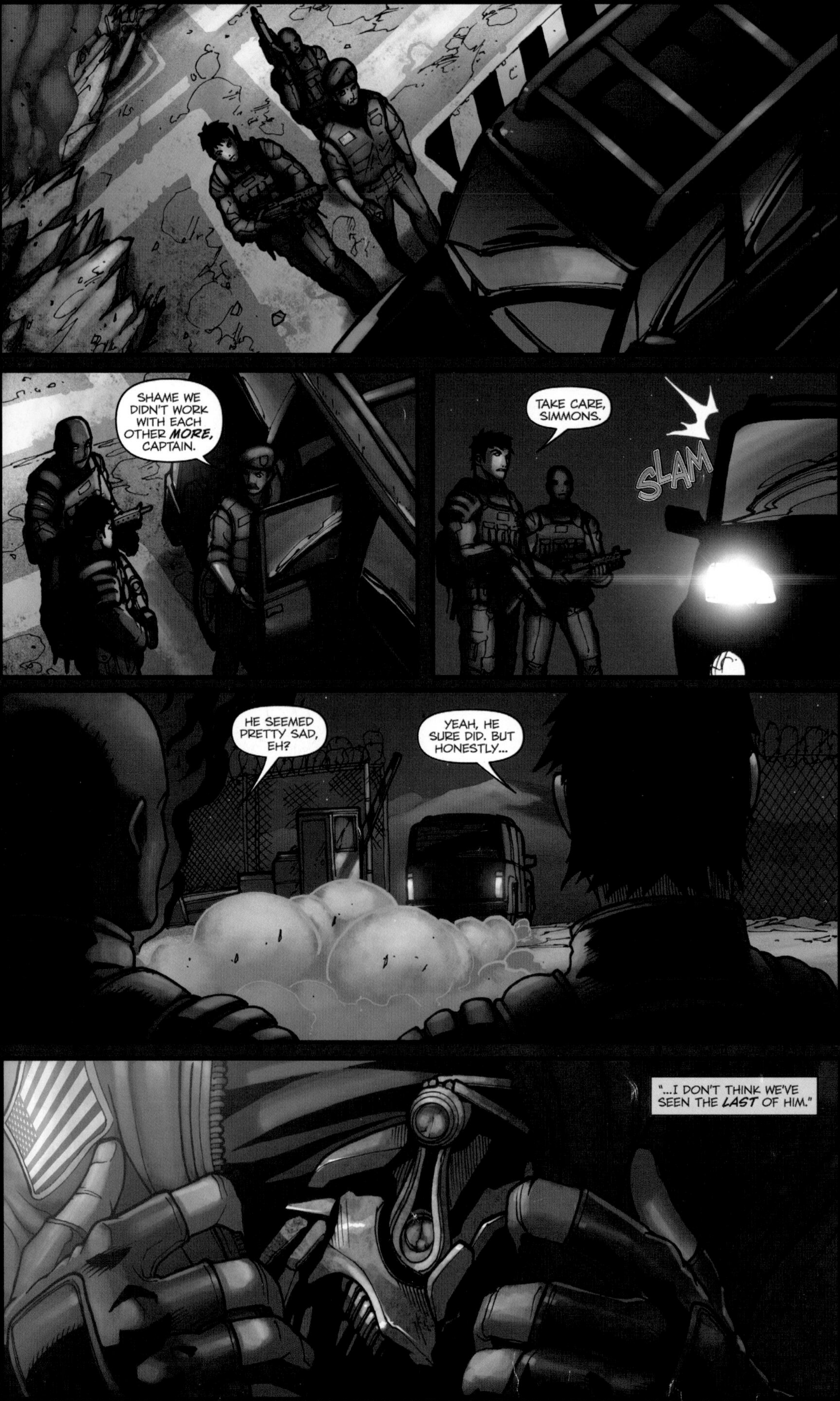
SHAME WE DIDN'T WORK WITH EACH OTHER MORE, CAPTAIN.
TAKE CARE, SIMMONS.
SLAM
HE SEEMED PRETTY SAD, EH?
YEAH, HE SURE DID. BUT HONESTLY...
"...I DON'T THINK WE'VE SEEN THE LAST OF HIM."

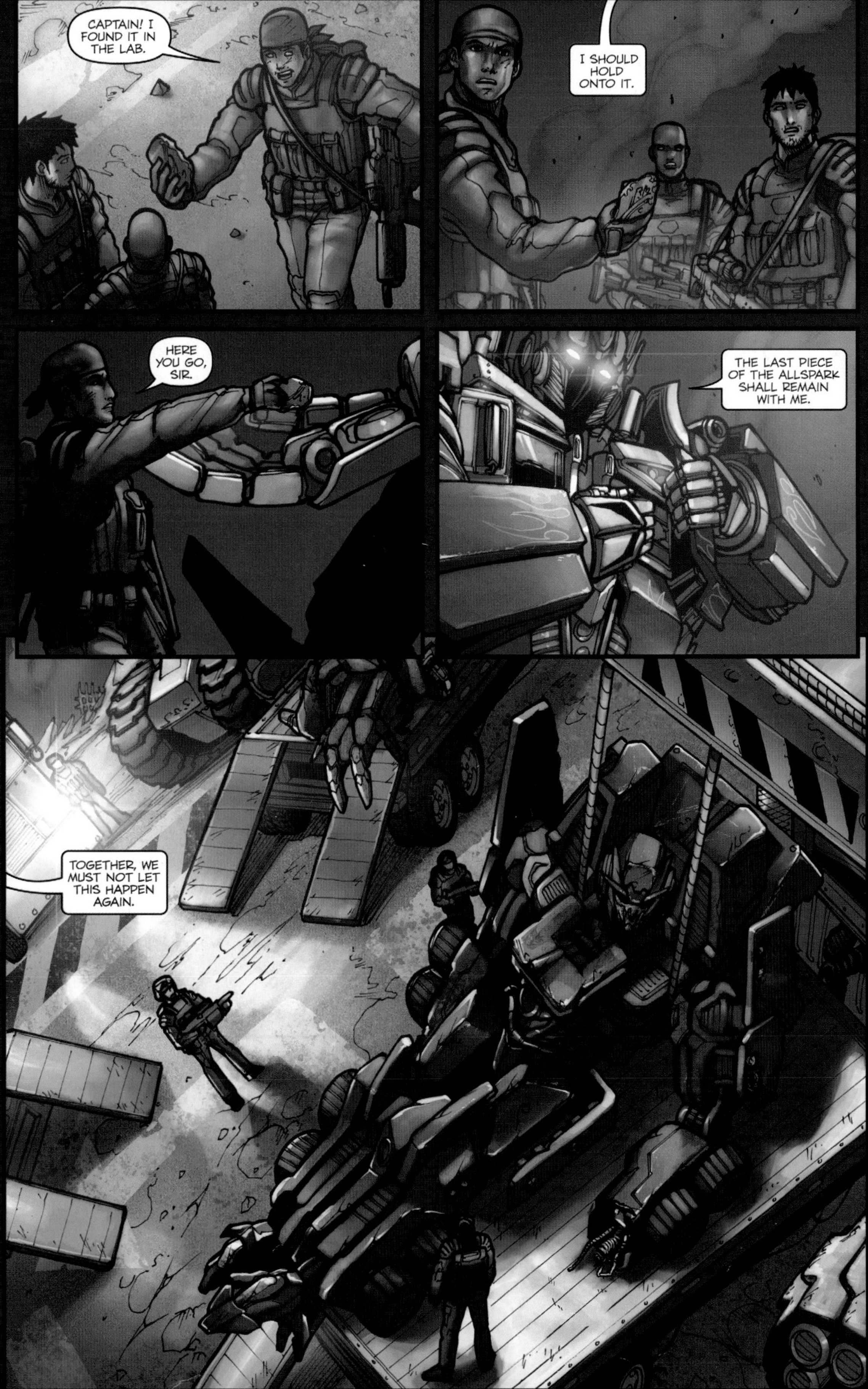
CAPTAIN! I FOUND IT IN THE LAB.
I SHOULD HOLD ONTO IT.
HERE YOU GO, SIR.
THE LAST PIECE OF THE ALLSPARK SHALL REMAIN WITH ME.
TOGETHER, WE MUST NOT LET THIS HAPPEN AGAIN.

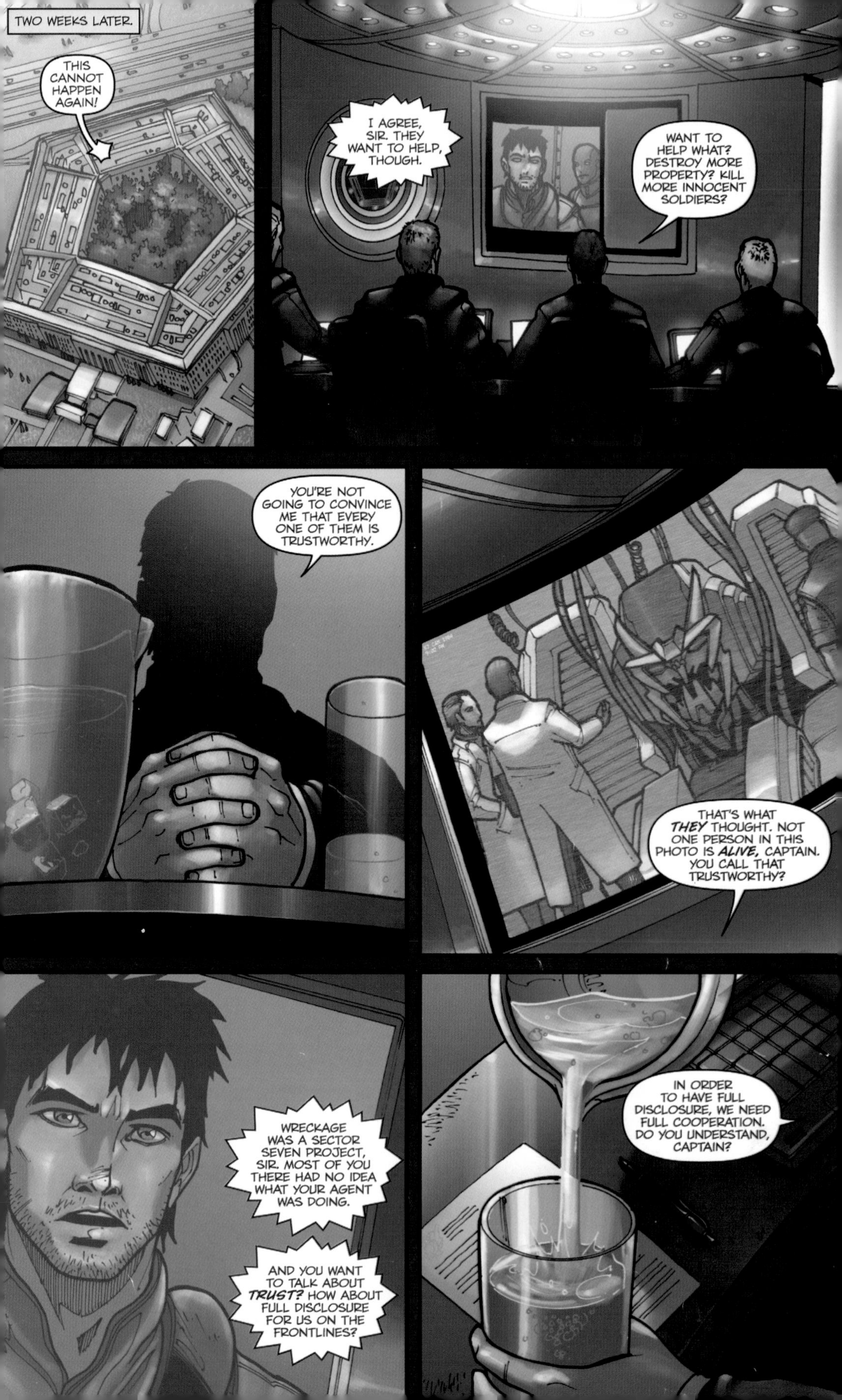
TWO WEEKS LATER.
THIS CANNOT HAPPEN AGAIN!
I AGREE, SIR. THEY WANT TO HELP, THOUGH.
WANT TO HELP WHAT? DESTROY MORE PROPERTY? KILL MORE INNOCENT SOLDIERS?
YOU'RE NOT GOING TO CONVINCE ME THAT EVERY ONE OF THEM IS TRUSTWORTHY.
THAT'S WHAT THEY THOUGHT. NOT ONE PERSON IN THIS PHOTO IS ALIVE, CAPTAIN. YOU CALL THAT TRUSTWORTHY?
WRECKAGE WAS A SECTOR SEVEN PROJECT, SIR. MOST OF YOU THERE HAD NO IDEA WHAT YOUR AGENT WAS DOING.
AND YOU WANT TO TALK ABOUT TRUST? HOW ABOUT FULL DISCLOSURE FOR US ON THE FRONTLINES?
IN ORDER TO HAVE FULL DISCLOSURE, WE NEED FULL COOPERATION. DO YOU UNDERSTAND, CAPTAIN?

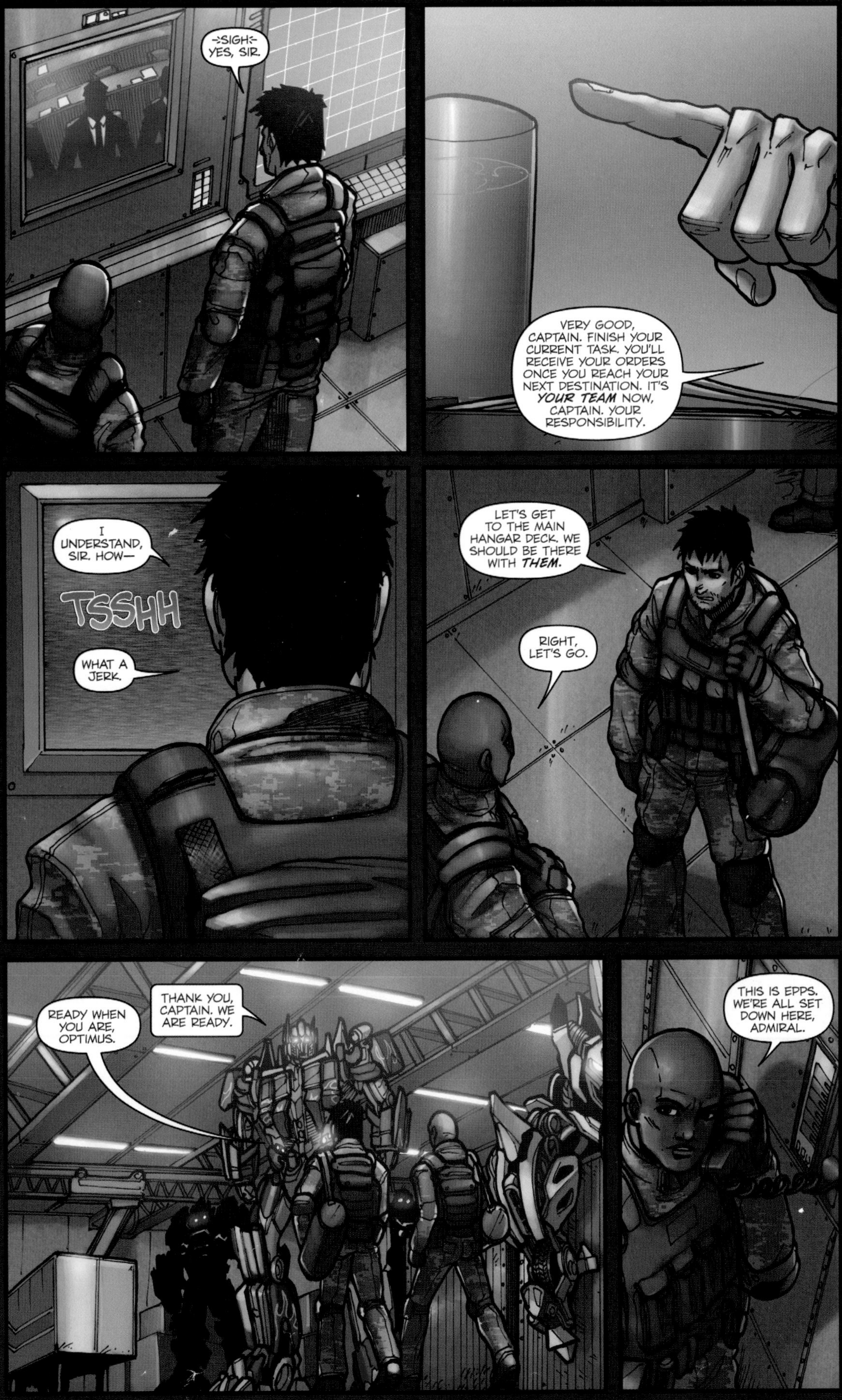
-SIGH- YES, SIR.
VERY GOOD, CAPTAIN. FINISH YOUR CURRENT TASK. YOU'LL RECEIVE YOUR ORDERS ONCE YOU REACH YOUR NEXT DESTINATION. IT'S YOUR TEAM NOW, CAPTAIN. YOUR RESPONSIBILITY.
I UNDERSTAND, SIR. HOW—
TSSHH
WHAT A JERK.
LET'S GET TO THE MAIN HANGAR DECK. WE SHOULD BE THERE WITH THEM.
RIGHT, LET'S GO.
READY WHEN YOU ARE, OPTIMUS.
THANK YOU, CAPTAIN. WE ARE READY.
THIS IS EPPS. WE'RE ALL SET DOWN HERE, ADMIRAL.

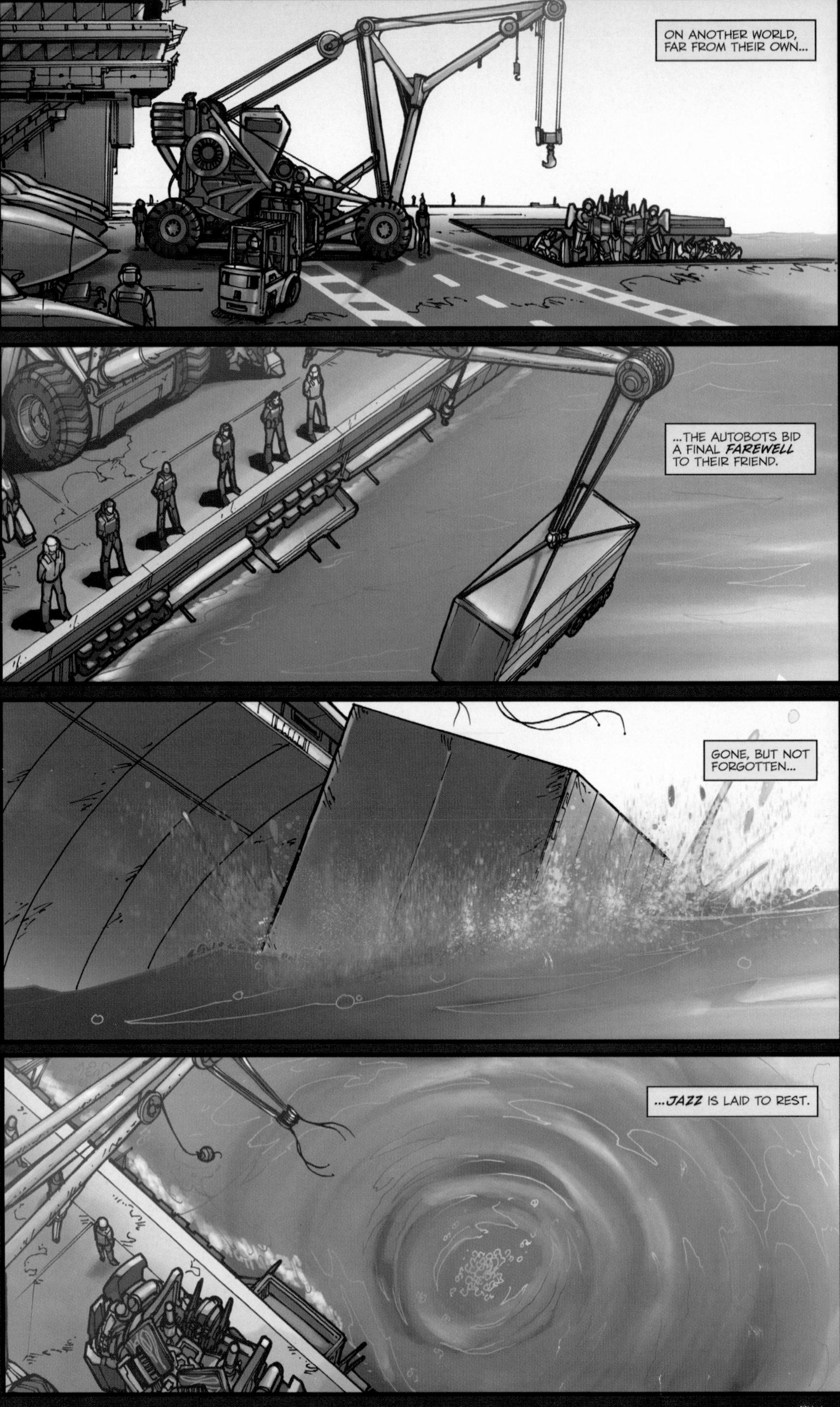
ON ANOTHER WORLD, FAR FROM THEIR OWN...
...THE AUTOBOTS BID A FINAL FAREWELL TO THEIR FRIEND.
GONE, BUT NOT FORGOTTEN...
...JAZZ IS LAID TO REST.

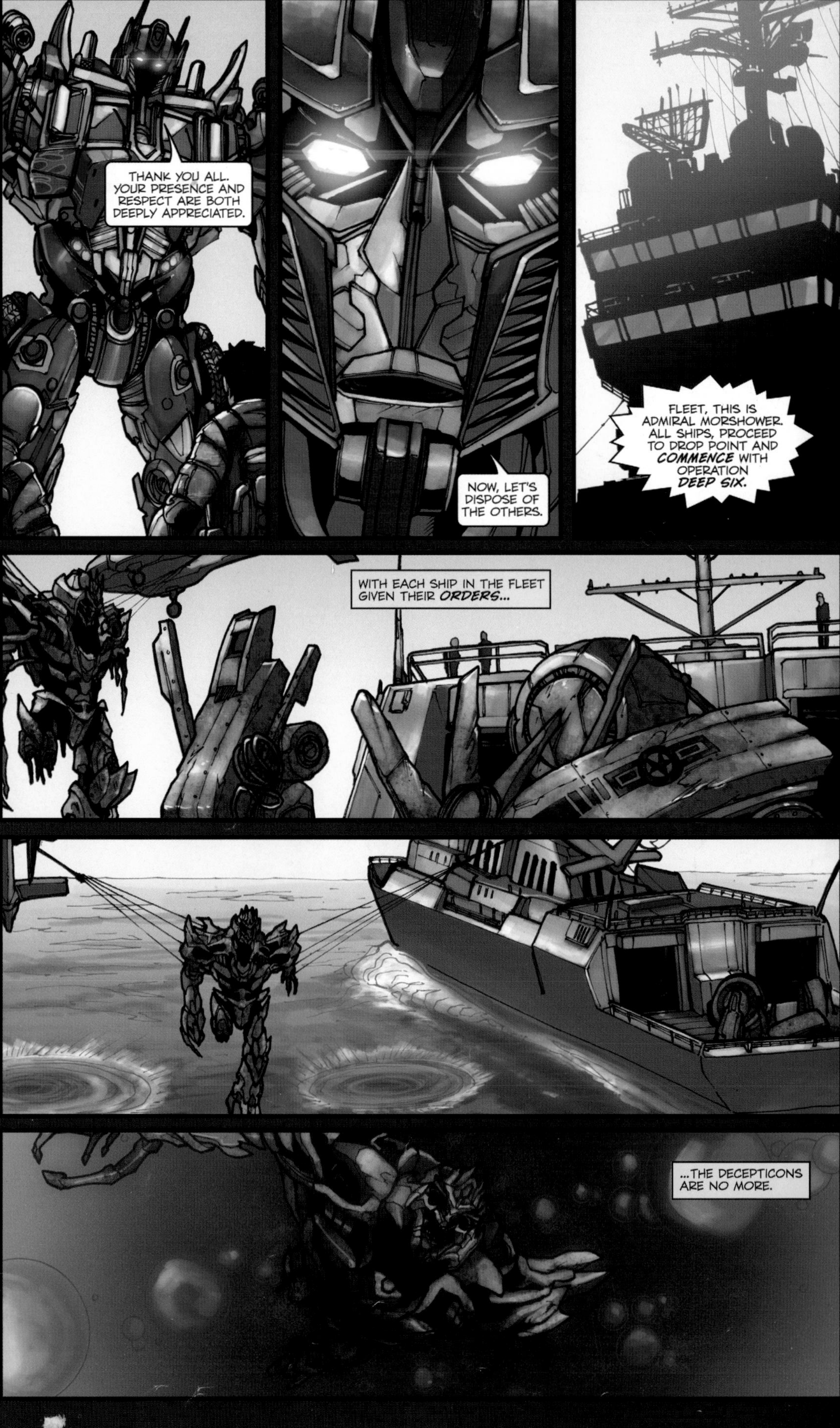
THANK YOU ALL. YOUR PRESENCE AND RESPECT ARE BOTH DEEPLY APPRECIATED.
NOW, LET'S DISPOSE OF THE OTHERS.
FLEET, THIS IS ADMIRAL MORSHOWER. ALL SHIPS, PROCEED TO DROP POINT AND COMMENCE WITH OPERATION DEEP SIX.
WITH EACH SHIP IN THE FLEET GIVEN THEIR ORDERS...
...THE DECEPTICONS ARE NO MORE.

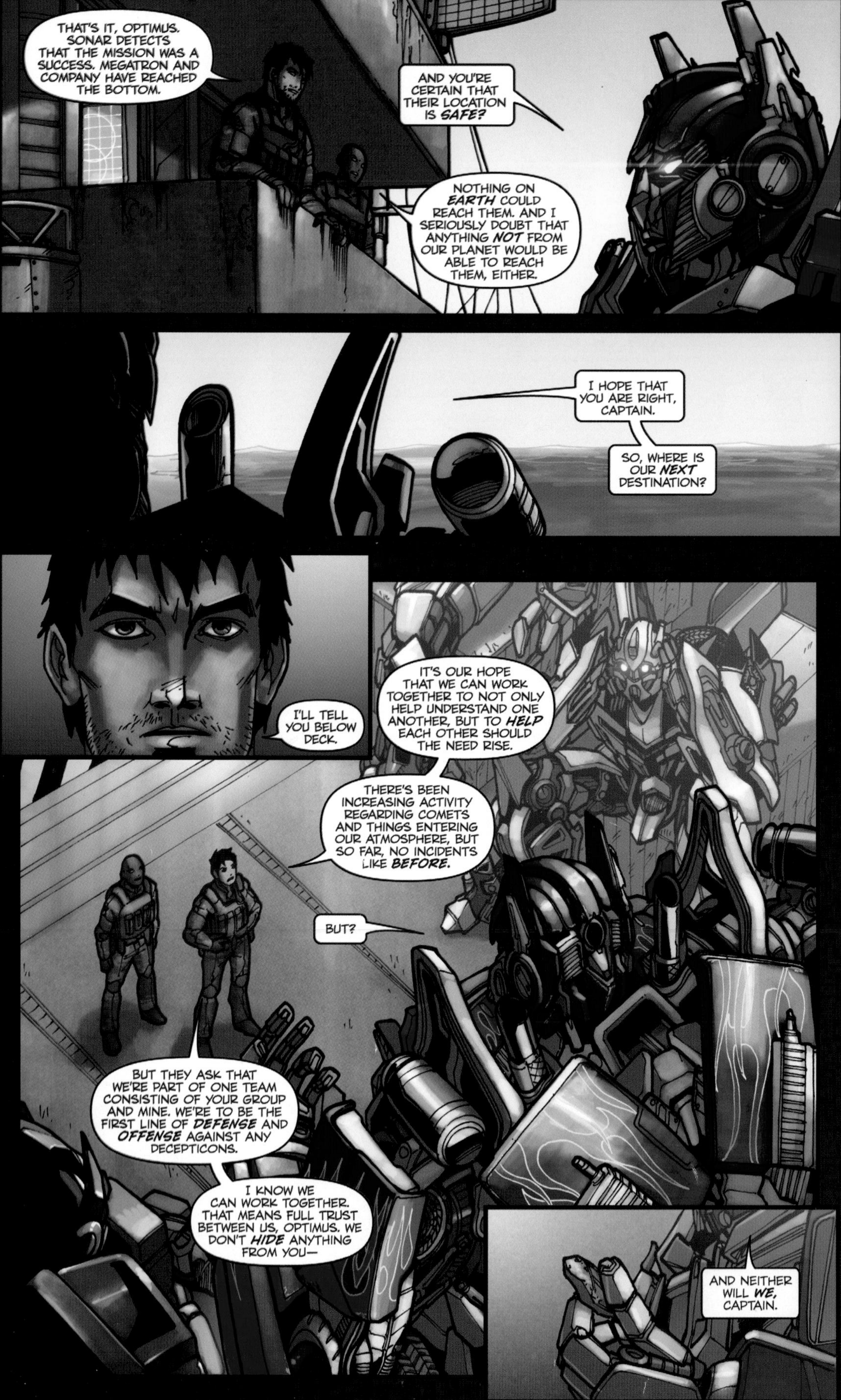
THAT'S IT, OPTIMUS. SONAR DETECTS THAT THE MISSION WAS A SUCCESS. MEGATRON AND COMPANY HAVE REACHED THE BOTTOM.
AND YOU'RE CERTAIN THAT THEIR LOCATION IS SAFE?
NOTHING ON EARTH COULD REACH THEM. AND I SERIOUSLY DOUBT THAT ANYTHING NOT FROM OUR PLANET WOULD BE ABLE TO REACH THEM, EITHER.
I HOPE THAT YOU ARE RIGHT, CAPTAIN.
SO, WHERE IS OUR NEXT DESTINATION?
I'LL TELL YOU BELOW DECK.
IT'S OUR HOPE THAT WE CAN WORK TOGETHER TO NOT ONLY HELP UNDERSTAND ONE ANOTHER, BUT TO HELP EACH OTHER SHOULD THE NEED RISE.
THERE'S BEEN INCREASING ACTIVITY REGARDING COMETS AND THINGS ENTERING OUR ATMOSPHERE, BUT SO FAR, NO INCIDENTS LIKE BEFORE.
BUT?
BUT THEY ASK THAT WE'RE PART OF ONE TEAM CONSISTING OF YOUR GROUP AND MINE. WE'RE TO BE THE FIRST LINE OF DEFENSE AND OFFENSE AGAINST ANY DECEPTICONS.
I KNOW WE CAN WORK TOGETHER. THAT MEANS FULL TRUST BETWEEN US, OPTIMUS. WE DON'T HIDE ANYTHING FROM YOU—
AND NEITHER WILL WE, CAPTAIN.

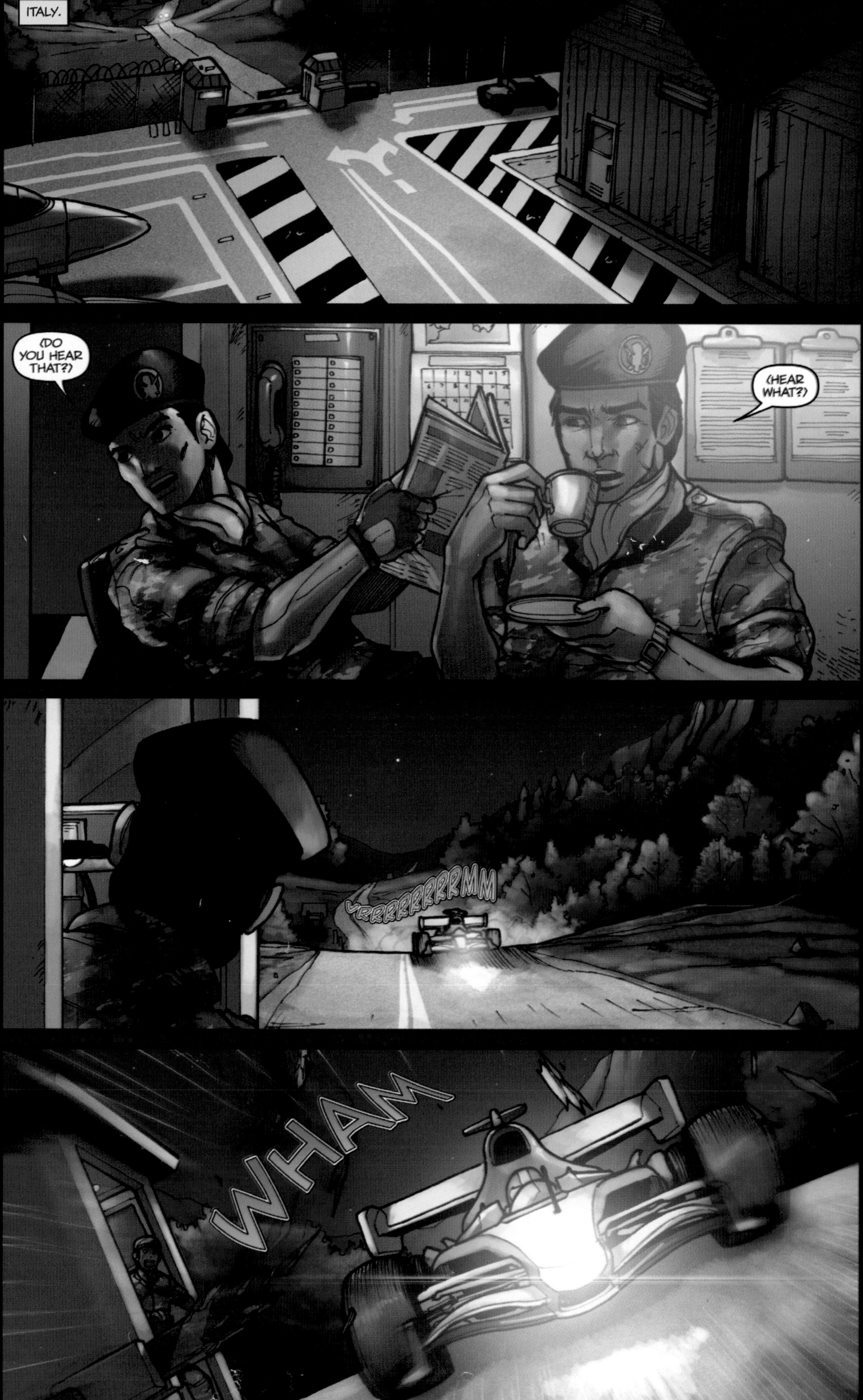
ITALY.
(DO YOU HEAR THAT?)
(HEAR WHAT?)
VRRRRRRRRRMM
WHAM

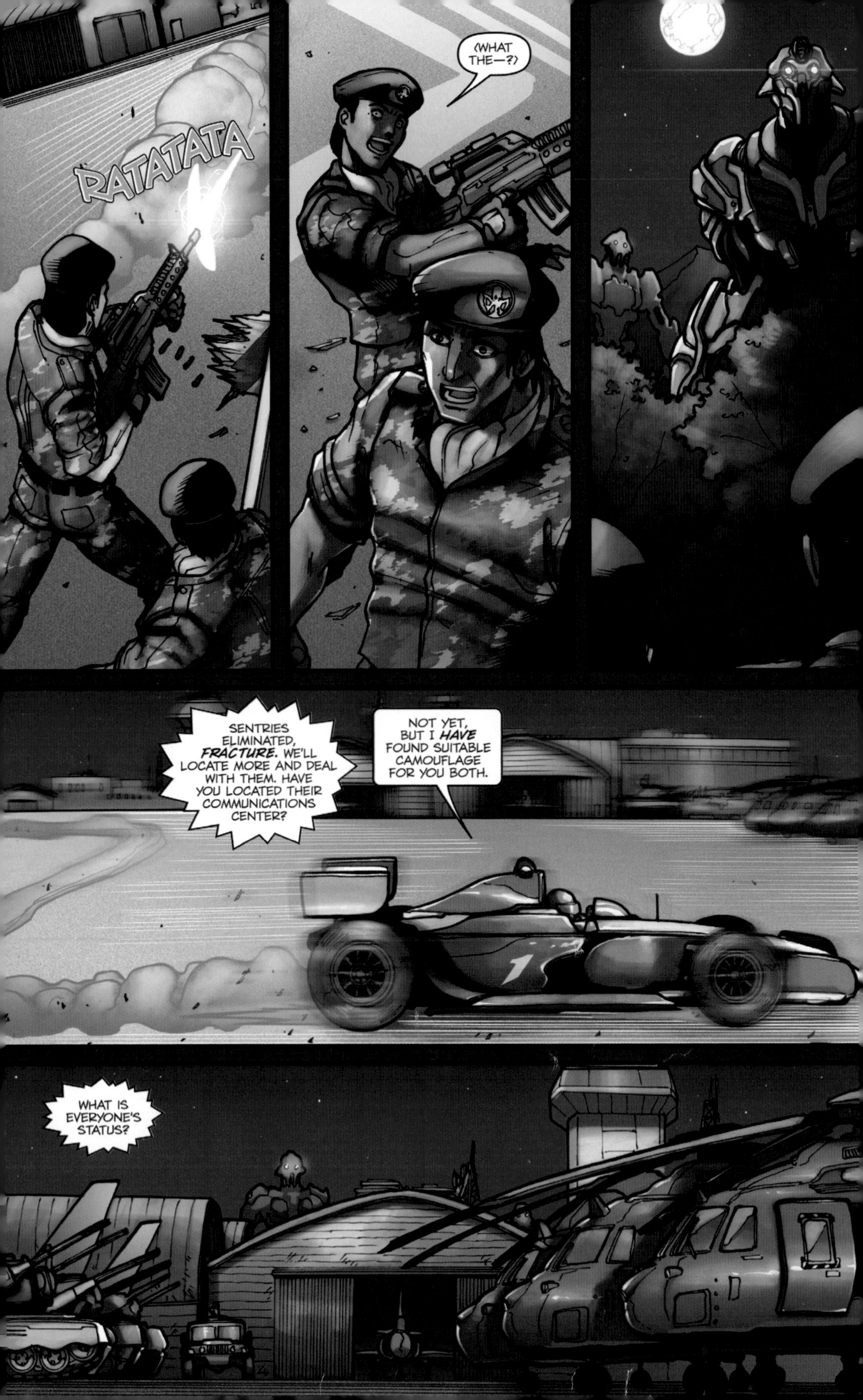
RATATATA
(WHAT THE—?)
SENTRIES ELIMINATED, FRACTURE. WE'LL LOCATE MORE AND DEAL WITH THEM. HAVE YOU LOCATED THEIR COMMUNICATIONS CENTER?
NOT YET, BUT I HAVE FOUND SUITABLE CAMOUFLAGE FOR YOU BOTH.
WHAT IS EVERYONE'S STATUS?

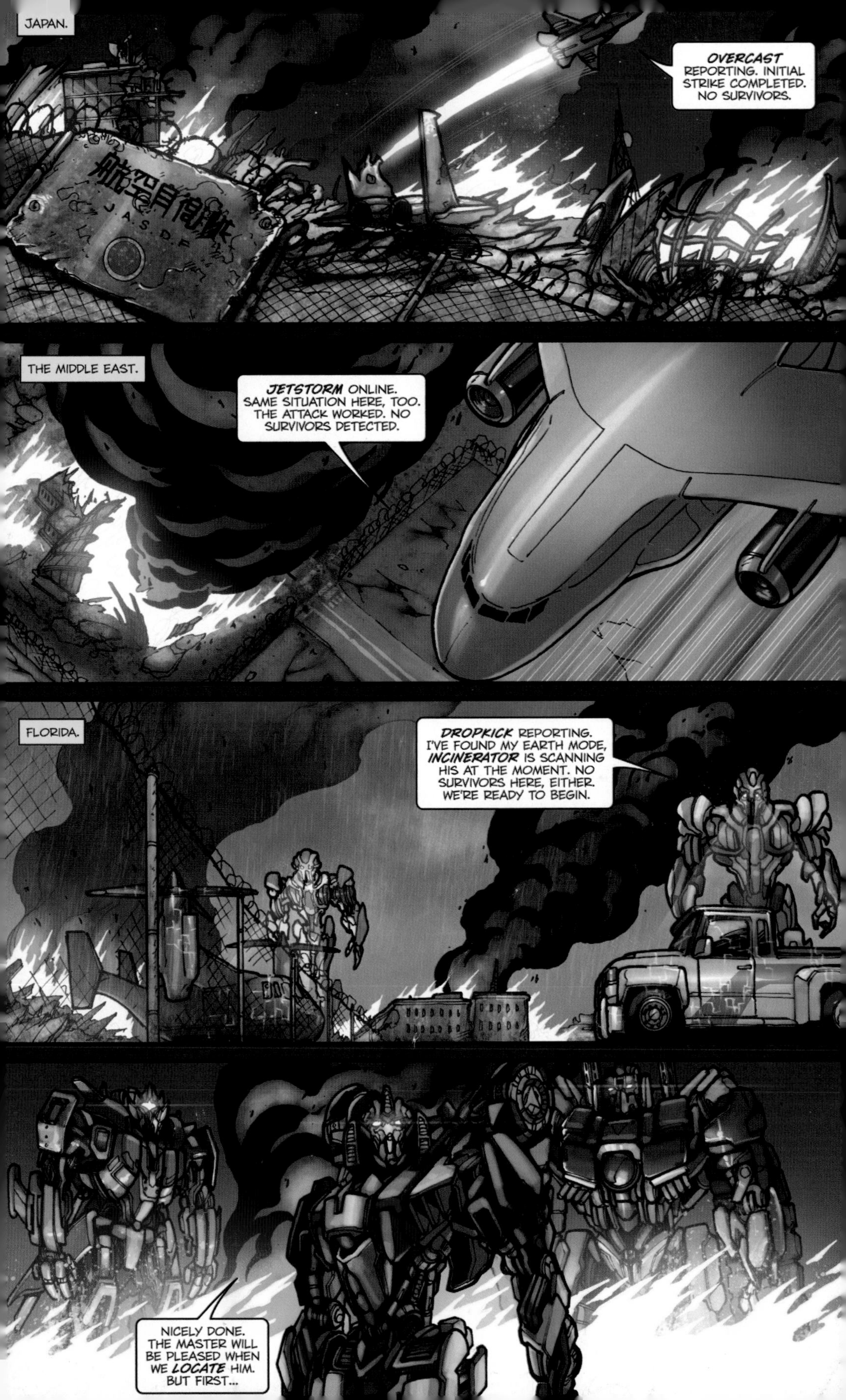
JAPAN.
航空自衛隊
J.A.S.D.F
OVERCAST REPORTING. INITIAL STRIKE COMPLETED. NO SURVIVORS.
THE MIDDLE EAST.
JETSTORM ONLINE. SAME SITUATION HERE, TOO. THE ATTACK WORKED. NO SURVIVORS DETECTED.
FLORIDA.
DROPKICK REPORTING. I'VE FOUND MY EARTH MODE, INCINERATOR IS SCANNING HIS AT THE MOMENT. NO SURVIVORS HERE, EITHER. WE'RE READY TO BEGIN.
NICELY DONE. THE MASTER WILL BE PLEASED WHEN WE LOCATE HIM. BUT FIRST...

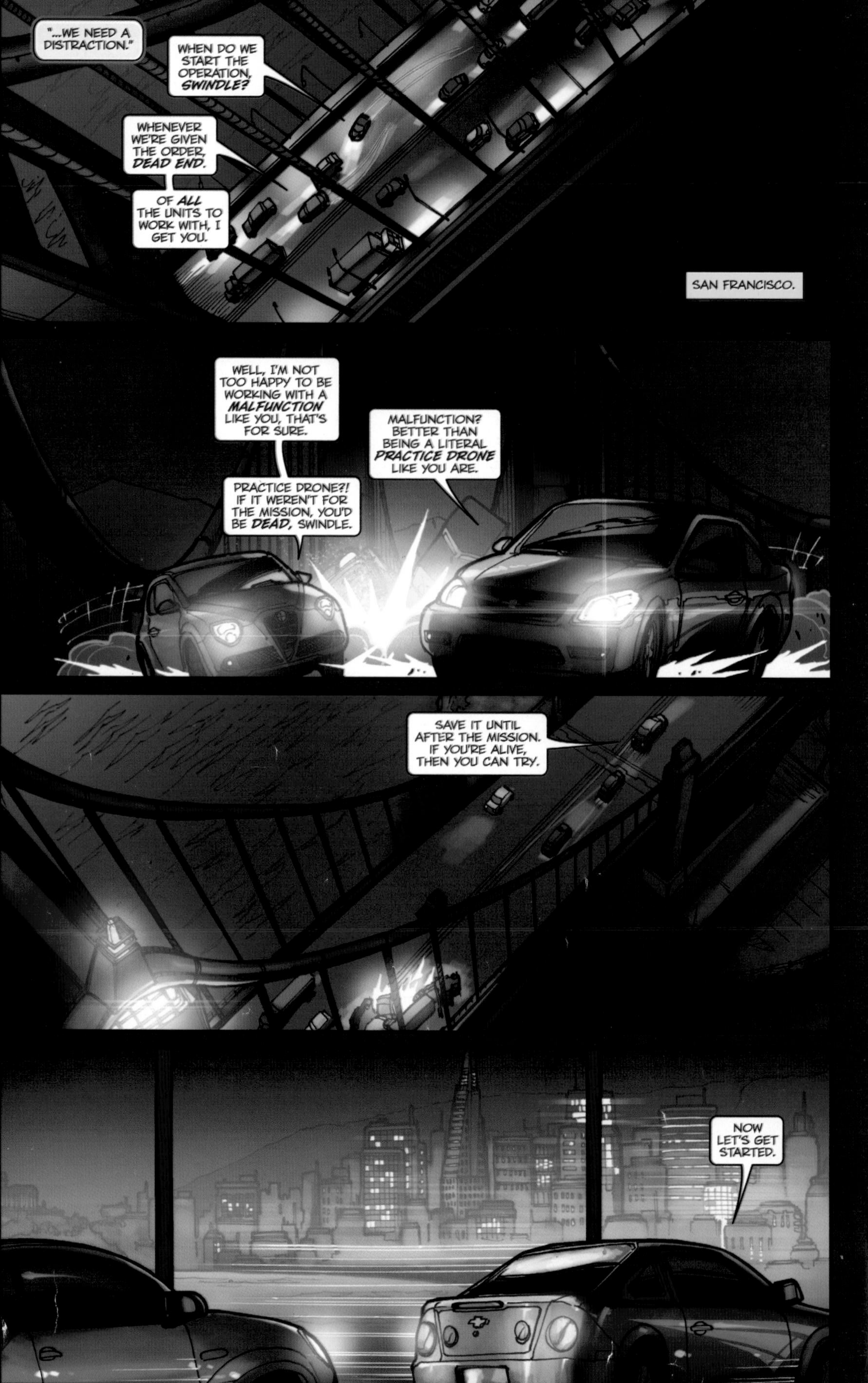
"...WE NEED A DISTRACTION."
WHEN DO WE START THE OPERATION, SWINDLE?
WHENEVER WE'RE GIVEN THE ORDER, DEAD END.
OF ALL THE UNITS TO WORK WITH, I GET YOU.
SAN FRANCISCO.
WELL, I'M NOT TOO HAPPY TO BE WORKING WITH A MALFUNCTION LIKE YOU, THAT'S FOR SURE.
MALFUNCTION? BETTER THAN BEING A LITERAL PRACTICE DRONE LIKE YOU ARE.
PRACTICE DRONE?! IF IT WEREN'T FOR THE MISSION, YOU'D BE DEAD, SWINDLE.
SAVE IT UNTIL AFTER THE MISSION. IF YOU'RE ALIVE, THEN YOU CAN TRY.
NOW LET'S GET STARTED.

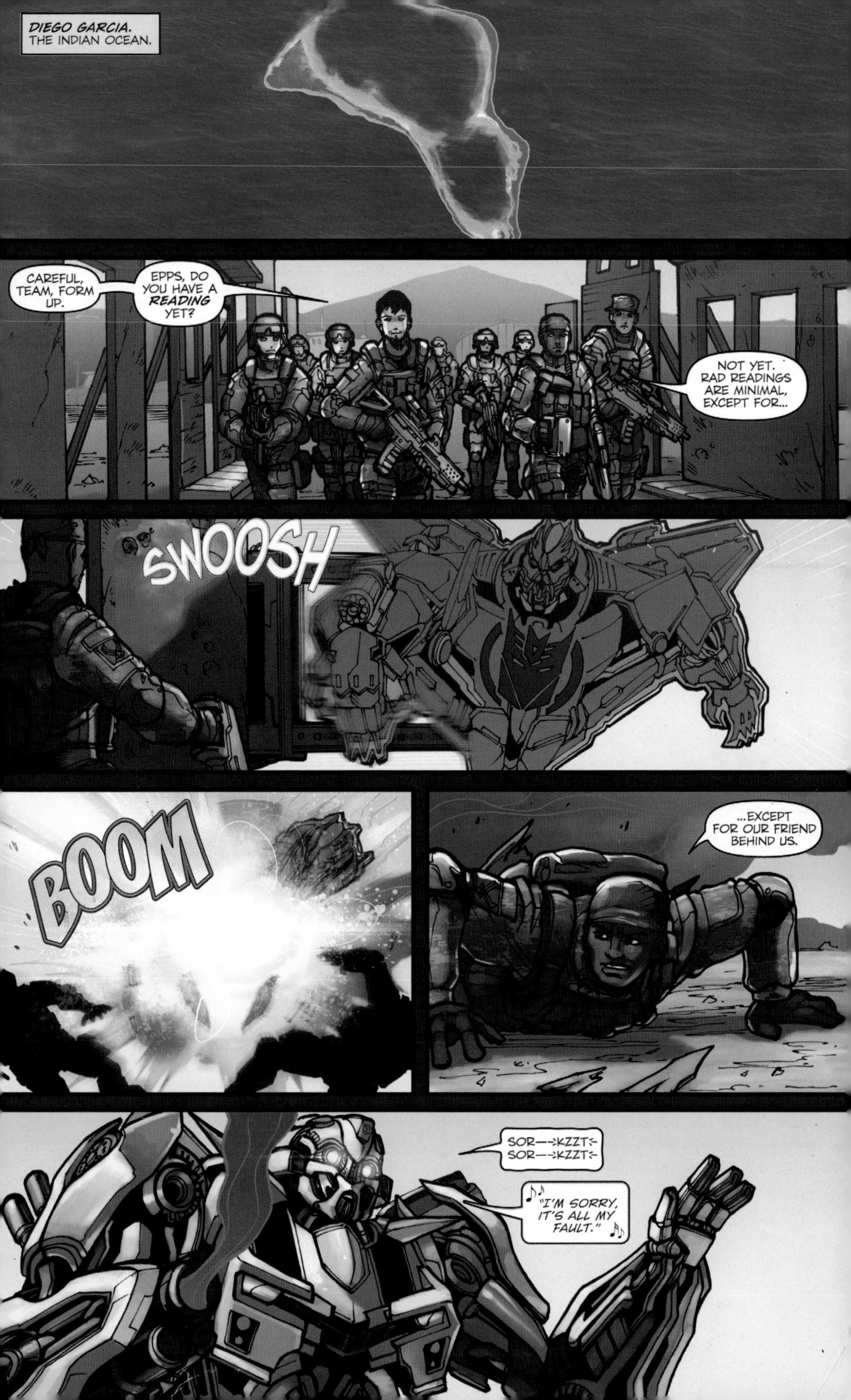
DIEGO GARCIA.
THE INDIAN OCEAN.
CAREFUL, TEAM, FORM UP.
EPPS, DO YOU HAVE A READING YET?
NOT YET. RAD READINGS ARE MINIMAL, EXCEPT FOR...
SWOOSH
BOOM
...EXCEPT FOR OUR FRIEND BEHIND US.
SOR--KZZT-
SOR--KZZT-
"I'M SORRY, IT'S ALL MY FAULT."

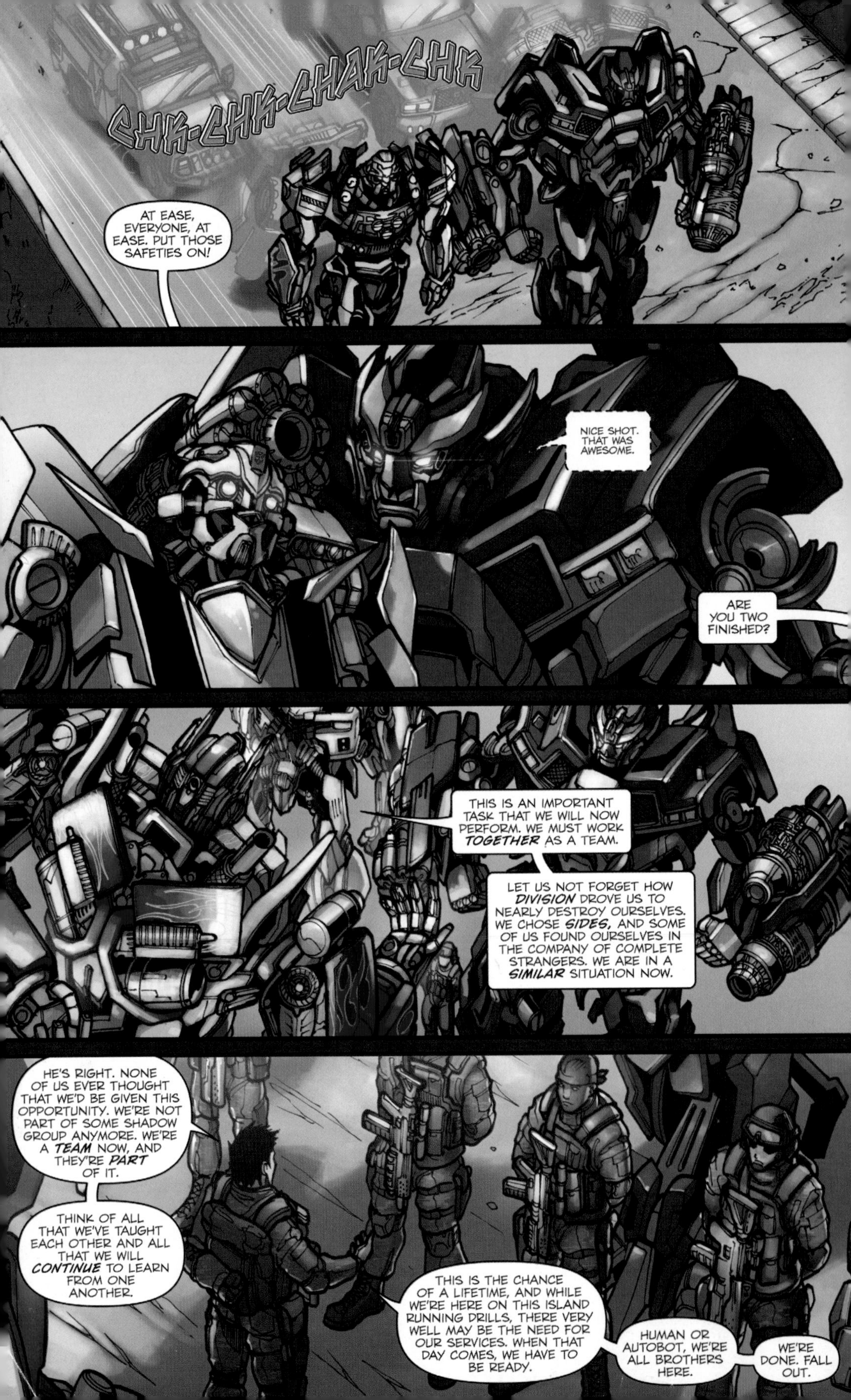
CHK-CHK-CHAK-CHK
AT EASE, EVERYONE, AT EASE. PUT THOSE SAFETIES ON!
NICE SHOT. THAT WAS AWESOME.
ARE YOU TWO FINISHED?
THIS IS AN IMPORTANT TASK THAT WE WILL NOW PERFORM. WE MUST WORK TOGETHER AS A TEAM.
LET US NOT FORGET HOW DIVISION DROVE US TO NEARLY DESTROY OURSELVES. WE CHOSE SIDES, AND SOME OF US FOUND OURSELVES IN THE COMPANY OF COMPLETE STRANGERS. WE ARE IN A SIMILAR SITUATION NOW.
HE'S RIGHT. NONE OF US EVER THOUGHT THAT WE'D BE GIVEN THIS OPPORTUNITY. WE'RE NOT PART OF SOME SHADOW GROUP ANYMORE. WE'RE A TEAM NOW, AND THEY'RE PART OF IT.
THINK OF ALL THAT WE'VE TAUGHT EACH OTHER AND ALL THAT WE WILL CONTINUE TO LEARN FROM ONE ANOTHER.
THIS IS THE CHANCE OF A LIFETIME, AND WHILE WE'RE HERE ON THIS ISLAND RUNNING DRILLS, THERE VERY WELL MAY BE THE NEED FOR OUR SERVICES. WHEN THAT DAY COMES, WE HAVE TO BE READY.
HUMAN OR AUTOBOT, WE'RE ALL BROTHERS HERE.
WE'RE DONE. FALL OUT.

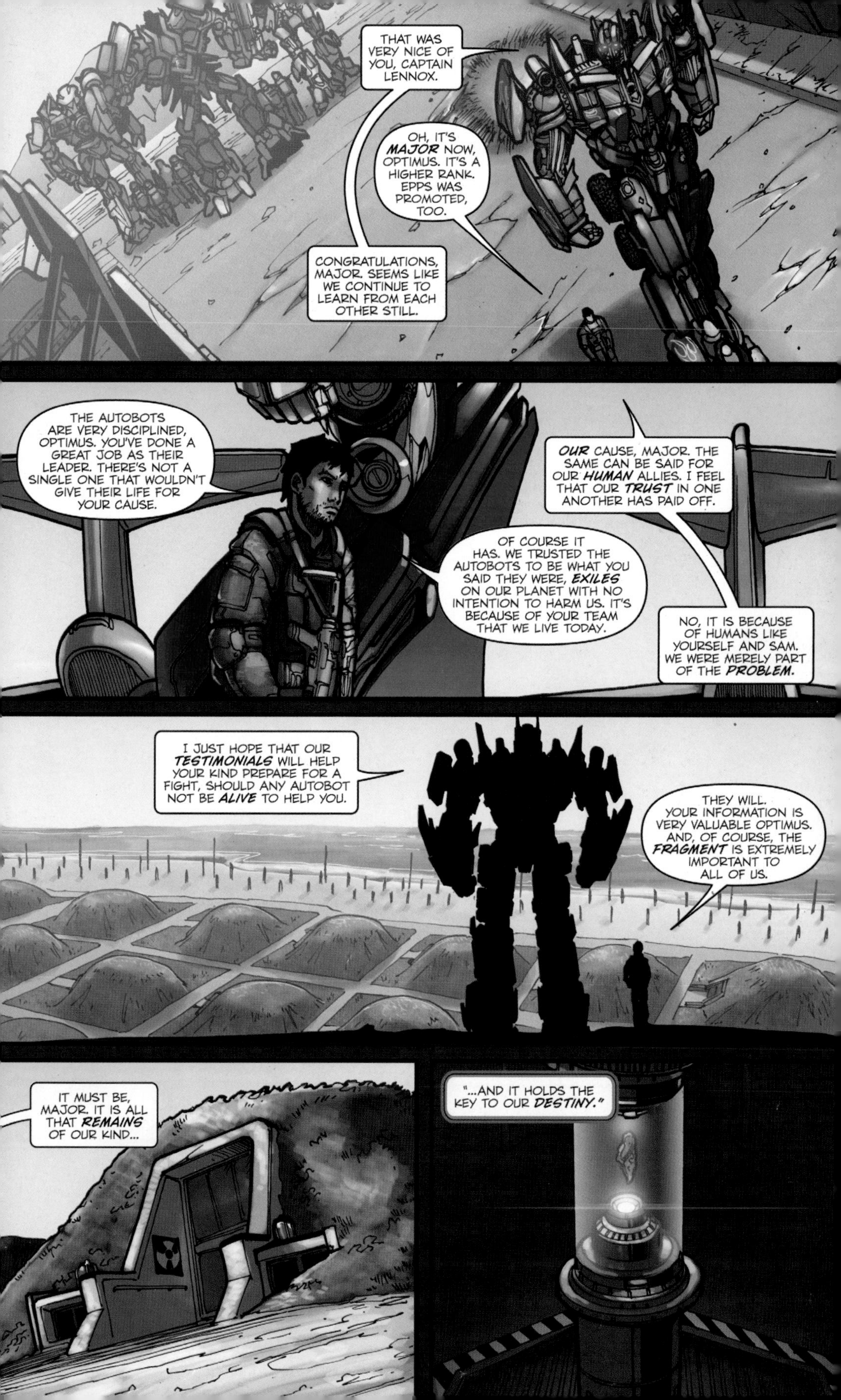

THAT WAS VERY NICE OF YOU, CAPTAIN LENNOX.
OH, IT'S MAJOR NOW, OPTIMUS. IT'S A HIGHER RANK. EPPS WAS PROMOTED, TOO.
CONGRATULATIONS, MAJOR. SEEMS LIKE WE CONTINUE TO LEARN FROM EACH OTHER STILL.
THE AUTOBOTS ARE VERY DISCIPLINED, OPTIMUS. YOU'VE DONE A GREAT JOB AS THEIR LEADER. THERE'S NOT A SINGLE ONE THAT WOULDN'T GIVE THEIR LIFE FOR YOUR CAUSE.
OUR CAUSE, MAJOR. THE SAME CAN BE SAID FOR OUR HUMAN ALLIES. I FEEL THAT OUR TRUST IN ONE ANOTHER HAS PAID OFF.
OF COURSE IT HAS. WE TRUSTED THE AUTOBOTS TO BE WHAT YOU SAID THEY WERE, EXILES ON OUR PLANET WITH NO INTENTION TO HARM US. IT'S BECAUSE OF YOUR TEAM THAT WE LIVE TODAY.
NO, IT IS BECAUSE OF HUMANS LIKE YOURSELF AND SAM. WE WERE MERELY PART OF THE PROBLEM.
I JUST HOPE THAT OUR TESTIMONIALS WILL HELP YOUR KIND PREPARE FOR A FIGHT, SHOULD ANY AUTOBOT NOT BE ALIVE TO HELP YOU.
THEY WILL. YOUR INFORMATION IS VERY VALUABLE OPTIMUS. AND, OF COURSE, THE FRAGMENT IS EXTREMELY IMPORTANT TO ALL OF US.
IT MUST BE, MAJOR. IT IS ALL THAT REMAINS OF OUR KIND...
"...AND IT HOLDS THE KEY TO OUR DESTINY."

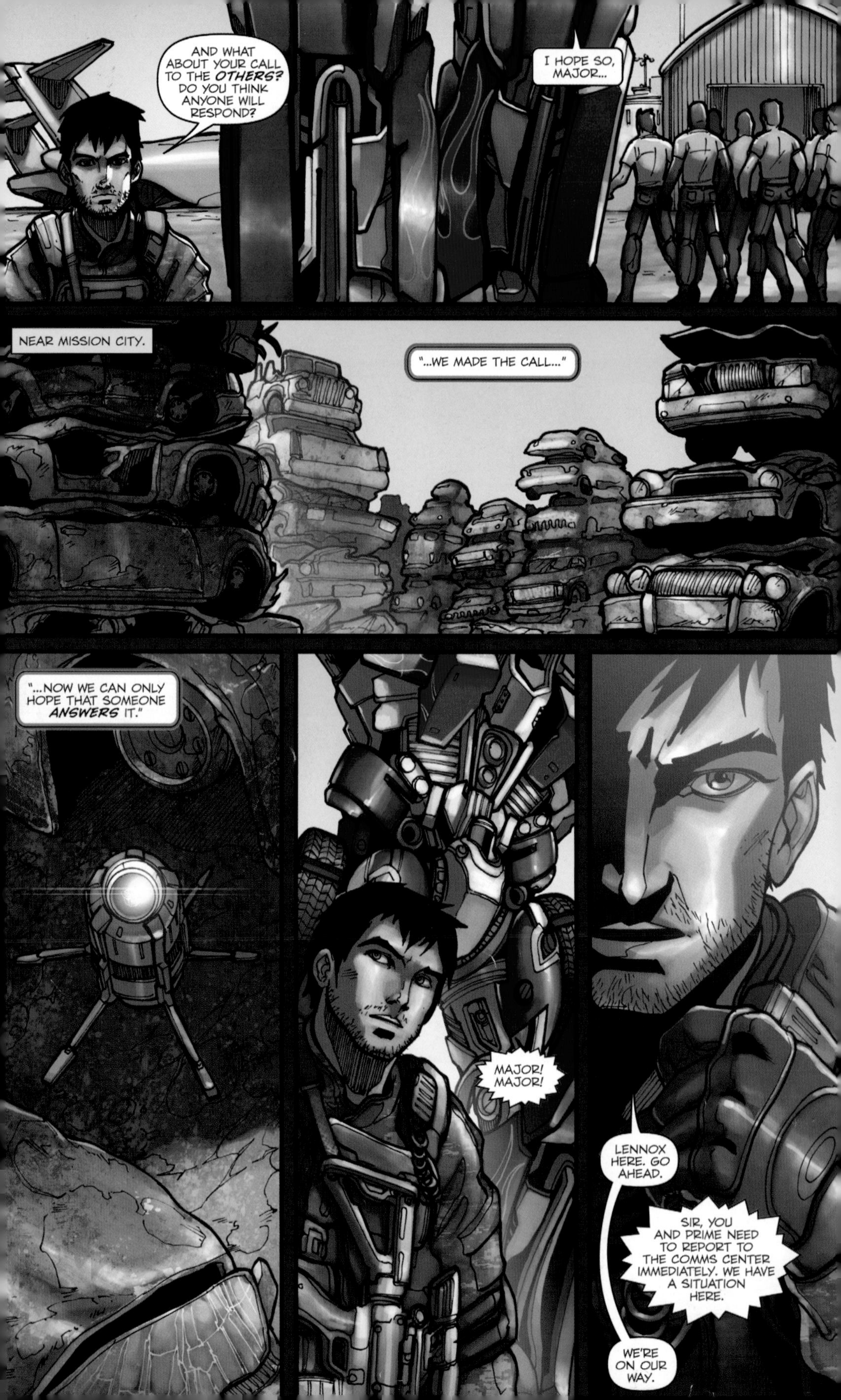
AND WHAT ABOUT YOUR CALL TO THE OTHERS? DO YOU THINK ANYONE WILL RESPOND?
I HOPE SO, MAJOR...
NEAR MISSION CITY.
"...WE MADE THE CALL..."
"...NOW WE CAN ONLY HOPE THAT SOMEONE ANSWERS IT."
MAJOR! MAJOR!
LENNOX HERE. GO AHEAD.
SIR, YOU AND PRIME NEED TO REPORT TO THE COMMS CENTER IMMEDIATELY. WE HAVE A SITUATION HERE.
WE'RE ON OUR WAY.

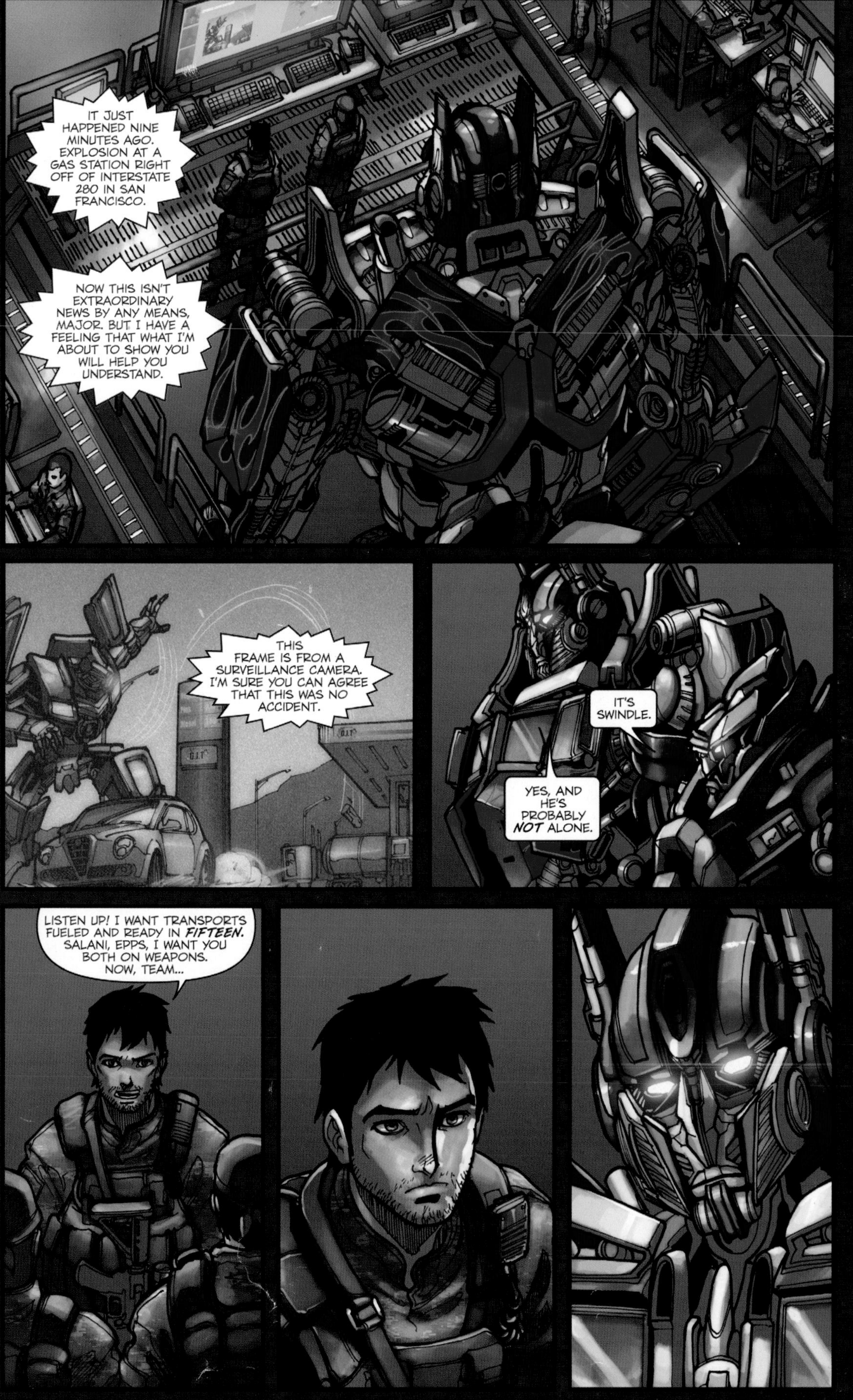
IT JUST HAPPENED NINE MINUTES AGO. EXPLOSION AT A GAS STATION RIGHT OFF OF INTERSTATE 280 IN SAN FRANCISCO.
NOW THIS ISN'T EXTRAORDINARY NEWS BY ANY MEANS, MAJOR. BUT I HAVE A FEELING THAT WHAT I'M ABOUT TO SHOW YOU WILL HELP YOU UNDERSTAND.
THIS FRAME IS FROM A SURVEILLANCE CAMERA. I'M SURE YOU CAN AGREE THAT THIS WAS NO ACCIDENT.
IT'S SWINDLE.
YES, AND HE'S PROBABLY ***NOT*** ALONE.
LISTEN UP! I WANT TRANSPORTS FUELED AND READY IN ***FIFTEEN.*** SALANI, EPPS, I WANT YOU BOTH ON WEAPONS. NOW, TEAM...

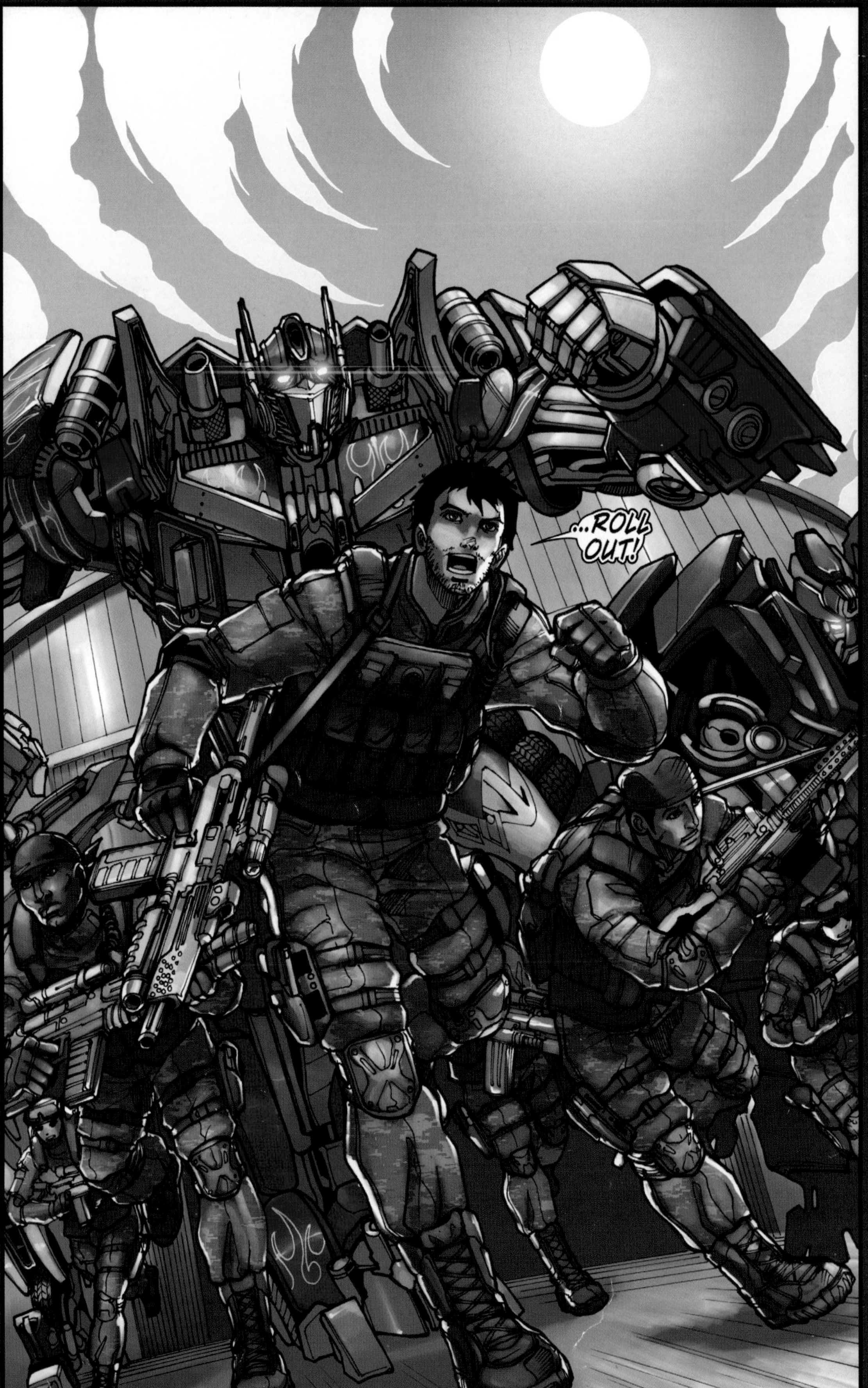
...ROLL OUT!